THE HOLIDAY INHERITANCE

DANA ISALY

PROLOGUE

FLORENCE

"Ren?" I hear my roommate toss her keys down in the bowl next to the front door as she calls out my name. I'm still in shock, staring down at the letter, when she walks into the living room. "Hey, you okay?"

I finally look up from the paper, and I'm sure my face betrays that I am not, in fact, okay.

"What's that?" She walks over to the couch and plops down next to me, her bright floral scent comforting me as it billows around us on the couch. When she grabs the letter out of my hands, I let her. Because I don't think I have it in me right now to explain what's going on. Is this what shock feels like?

"Florence Anne Donahue," she begins, reading the letter I've been rereading for hours now. "We here at Smith & Jones Solicitors are reaching out on behalf of your late great-aunt Katharine Clemonte. Fancy name," she says, nudging me with her elbow. I'm still unmoving as she continues. "As you are the last surviving member of her extended family, she has left her entire estate to you. This includes her country home in Yorkshire, all of her possessions, and a substantial amount of capital."

When Amie looks up, I look over to meet her gaze. She looks just as shocked as I feel. I shrug, and she continues with the rest of the letter.

"Due to the laws around estates in the United Kingdom, we need to get in touch with you as soon as possible to make all of the proper arrangements for the transfer of ownership and funds. You have six months to respond and make plans to travel before the government will, unfortunately, take control of the estate. Please reach out to us at your earliest convenience. We are sorry for your loss and hope that this letter finds you well."

Amie scoffs. "This *has* to be a scam. Right? This is like a new version of the Nigerian princes trying to get money from old people."

"Actually," I tell her, finally finding my voice, "it's not." I take it back from her hands, running my fingers over the typed font. "I looked them up on the internet, and they're real. So I decided to reach out because I figured someone was using their business name to scam people. I got an email back within an hour explaining that it's all true and that they need me to fly over as soon as I possibly can."

Her jaw drops, and I can tell she's trying to think of something to say. But this has clearly knocked her on her ass as well. How can it not? Who the hell gets letters about a deceased aunt who has left an entire fortune to you? Characters in movies, that's who. Not broke-ass waitresses who can barely afford rent.

"This. Is. Amazing!" She squeals and jumps up off the couch, tugging me up off my ass with her. "You're rich! Holy shit, Ren. You are fucking *rich*! You have a whole estate! When can you move in? How does the citizenship thing work with this? Can you bring a friend? Asking for a friend. It's me. I'm the friend."

"Oh, my god, Amie!" I laugh as she continues to dance around the coffee table. "You're going to piss off the downstairs neighbors again."

"Who gives a fuck?" She runs back over to me, grabbing my hands as her blue eyes sparkle with all the joy she's feeling right now. "We're moving to England!"

"We?" I ask, raising an eyebrow in her direction. Of course I'm going to take her with me, but I have to give her some shit for it first. "Who said anything about *we*?"

"Oh, shut up. You know you have to take me! I'm basically a sister!"

"You *are* a sister." Amie and I have been friends since we were fifteen, and when my parents died six years ago, she officially took up the role of family, seeing as I didn't have any left. We've been inseparable since. "Of course you have to come with me. I cannot do this alone."

She bites her lip, holding back a huge smile I know she wants to let loose. "How much money do you think it is? Hundreds of thousands? Millions?"

"Not a clue. They weren't super forthcoming on email just because of all the legal things that go along with it, I guess? God, I'm terrified."

"Of? How can you be terrified? This is huge, Ren. This is everything you could've ever asked for. It sounds like you're going to be set for life. Who cares if you have to move to England for it to happen?"

"Because this is insane. This shit happens in movies, not in real life."

"It just hasn't sunk in yet," she tells me, looking far more confident than I feel. "You'll get excited once we buy the tickets."

"God, my credit card is going to weep." I sink back down onto the couch and let the butterflies in my stomach flutter around.

"Not for long!" Amie sings, prancing around the room once again. "You're rich, bitch!"

CHAPTER ONE
FLORENCE

Standing in line at customs is probably the single most terrifying thing I've ever had to do. The first time I came through with Amie, all was well. All I had to do was tell them we were here about an inheritance and to meet with solicitors. The lady behind the glass smiled, stamped my passport, and let me through. Easy peasy.

But this time is different. This time, I'm coming through with a temporary visa, official letters from the solicitors, and all of my inheritance paperwork. I'll have to tell them I'm here to *live*, not just to visit. Mr. Smith, the solicitor my great-aunt hired, has assured me that I have everything I need to get in and live here until the rest of my paperwork goes through. I have his number in my pocket just in case anything goes wrong.

I've seen those border shows, though, and while I'm not carrying or doing anything illegal, it still scares the shit out of me that they could detain me or turn me right back around. I've packed up my entire life—three suitcases and a carry-on—and Amie and I have broken the lease to our apartment. So this is something that is happening. If they were to turn me around, I wouldn't really have anywhere to go.

I wish Amie was here. I get it, she needed to spend the Christmas holidays with her family back in New York, but I'm selfish and want her here for comfort. She'll be flying over after the New Year, though, and staying with me for a few months while her student visa gets processed. She's been accepted into a local university and has decided to go back and get her master's degree. Me, on the other hand, I have no clue what I'm going to do once I get settled.

I've been told the country home and grounds are taken care of by a few people who have worked on the home for years. I guess Aunt Katharine wrote in her will that they were to have jobs as long as they wanted, which isn't an issue for me. I've never even lived in a place with a yard, so I don't think I could even start a lawnmower, let alone take care of acres and acres of land.

"Next!" the gentleman behind the glass shouts in my direction. Sweat pebbles on my forehead, and I push the sleeves of my sweater up off my forearms. Why is it so freaking hot in here?

"Hi there," I say, plastering on my sweetest smile.

The man just takes my documentation, not looking

up from the desk in front of him. "Purpose of your visit?"

He finds the picture on my passport and then again on my visa and holds it up as if to check I'm who I say I am.

"Inheritance. Um, sorry. I inherited my aunt's estate, and I'm here to officially move in!" A laugh that sounds half-manic escapes my lips, and I immediately flush hot with embarrassment.

Jesusfuckingchrist.

After several more questions, every single paper read through, and with what looks like a begrudged smile, he lets me go, wishing me luck as he does so. I practically sprint to checked baggage, praying under my breath that all of my luggage has made it. My boots are heavy and hot. I don't know why I thought it was a good idea to dress for the snow, even though I'd be spending most of my day inside airports and planes. I'm about ready to strip down a few layers when I see a man holding a sign with my name on it. "Miss Donahue" is written in scrawled black permanent marker on a thin sheet of printer paper.

Nothing but the best, I guess? Honestly, I was expecting Mr. Smith to pick me up, but I must've misunderstood his emails. The man standing there with the sign looks to be in his mid-forties, with warm brown hair and a beard flecked with gray. He's tall and broad and looks like he knows how to swing an ax in that flannel shirt. As I approach him, he catches my eye and looks surprised.

"Are you here for me?" I ask, dipping under the roped divider between us.

"You aren't supposed to do that," he says, ignoring me altogether. His voice is deep, and the closer I get to him, the more I can take him in. His eyes are a deep, rich brown that seem to shine even in the fluorescents of the airport. And he smells so good. My god, what is that? He smells exactly like a man should, spicy and sweet all at once.

"Oh, sorry. I just thought… I mean, you're right here. Sorry, are you here for me?"

"Is your name Miss Donahue?"

"Yes."

He clears his throat and blinks a few times. "Then, yes. I'm here for you. Do you have luggage?" He begins to lead me toward baggage claim, and I follow behind at quite a clip as I try to keep up. His long legs propel him far ahead of me.

"Quite a bit," I admit, breathless, my face flushing again. The sweat is dripping down my back now, and between being so hot and being so nervous about this whole ordeal while also being surrounded by too many loud people, I'm about to have a breakdown. I'm so overstimulated and out of my depth that I could cry. And why is this fucking sweater so goddamn itchy?

"I assumed," he grunts over his shoulder. When he sees that I'm struggling to keep up, his face softens, and he stops until I've caught up. His hand reaches out and takes the backpack off my shoulder, slinging it over his own with ease. "That was rude of me," he says. "I should've offered to carry this for you. I'm sure you're exhausted."

"Thanks. Yeah, it's been a long day. I'm just ready for a bath and sleep." We begin walking again, this time slower. I can tell it bothers him as he continues to glance down at me, but it's not like my legs can just magically grow a few inches. "I figured Mr. Smith would be picking me up."

"The solicitor?" He laughs, the sound rich and comforting. "He's not taking time away from his family during the holidays to pick up a client. You're stuck with me, I'm afraid."

"What was your name? Are you an associate of his or?"

"Briggs Davies." When he looks down at me this time, his dark eyebrows are pulled together. "They didn't tell you? I'm the head groundskeeper. I'm the one that keeps the place going."

"Oh, wow! Okay, no. They didn't tell me. I was sad we didn't get to meet last time I was here. I'm Florence, but you can call me Ren. Nice to meet you." I hold out my hand, clammy as it may be. His calloused hand wraps around my own, and I have to fight against my wild hormones that have suddenly taken an interest in this growly older man.

"Florence," he says, nodding as we go back to

watching bags circle the conveyor belt. "That's an old name."

I shrug. "Family name. I'm the fifth woman on my mom's side to have the name. Briggs is unique. I haven't heard that one before. Is it an English name?"

"And Scottish. Think it actually goes back to Norse, but I'm not sure."

We wait in silence for a while longer until my bags finally show up. They're old, purchased secondhand last minute when I realized just how much stuff I was going to be bringing. Briggs jogs over to the baggage carts and grabs us one before lifting them all with ease onto it. I can't help but watch the way his shoulders and arms bulge against the soft fabric of his flannel. And with each movement, I catch a whiff of his cologne.

"Shall we?" he asks once all of my luggage is loaded. Embarrassed that he probably just caught me smelling him, all I do is nod and gesture for him to lead the way. The bitterly cold air whacks me straight across my face when the automatic doors part, and it slices easily through my sweater. Seeing as I was sweaty just moments ago, it's almost painfully cold.

"We're just right here!" he calls out over the wind. Snow is coming down, wet and thick, landing heavily on my luggage and our hair. "Lucked out with the spot."

I try my hardest not to stare at his ass in those sinfully tight jeans as he walks ahead of me, leading the way. It doesn't really work, though, because when he stops in front of his impressively well-kept old Land

Rover, I bump right into his back. *Embarrassing*. The Rover is a sage green with a white top, and frankly, it looks like this snowstorm could blow it away. The metal, while solid, seems thin and flimsy up close, and I'm wondering if it's actually safe to get in.

On the hood—or bonnet, I should say—is a spare tire with white walls, just like the other four. Along with the tire, there are two long side mirrors that stick up and back toward the driver and passenger-side door. *Odd place to put those.*

"Hop in, little duck. I'll get the old lady started." He pats the bonnet and smiles warmly at it, like it's a living creature.

The door creaks when I open it, and my anxieties are not eased. But the old thing cranks to life, and hot air almost immediately starts blowing out of its vents. I hop up, eager to get warm again, while Briggs loads up the back of the car. I take the time to look around while he's occupied, running my fingers over the bumps on the dash and toying with the buttons. The front has bucket seats, but in the back, it has benches against the long outer windows.

No seat belts. Cool. *Great*.

"It's really coming down out there," he says as a blast of cold air enters the cabin before his own creaky door slams shut.

"I hope we can make it back to the house." I worry my lip as I stare out the windshield.

"Don't you worry, little duck. I'll get us back." The

Rover jolts as he throws it in reverse, and my hands fly out to catch purchase on anything near. I'm jittery and tired from the copious amounts of caffeine I've been slamming back, and I'm not completely convinced *any* of this was a good idea right about now.

He glances at me but otherwise says nothing. "Are you calling me a duck?"

A sexy-as-hell grin peeks out, forcing a dimple in one cheek. "Just a little nickname around here. Like *love* or *lass*."

I nod and turn to stare out the window while he navigates the airport parking lot, then the highways. The snow continues to come down, and the roads turn to slush. He's driving slowly, but I'm still nervous. I don't like not having a seatbelt.

Suddenly, a wave of emotion hits me, and I have to bite back the tears. It came on so rapidly that I didn't even register what it was until tears were collecting on my lashes. I'm all alone in a country I've only ever visited once. I don't know a single soul, and it's Christmas. Why did I decide to go down this road? I could've sold the whole thing, taking all the money and living for the rest of my life off the legacy of the great-aunt I never met.

But no. I had to choose the adventurous one. The one that meant I had to move here *before* the year was up. The one that meant I was going to be alone and depressed on Christmas. And in a snowstorm. What happens if I get snowed in and I can't get out to get food? I don't even have a car.

What the fuck am I doing?

CHAPTER TWO
FLORENCE

WHEN WE PULL up to my new home, I can finally release a stress-filled breath. I've been white-knuckling it on the holy-shit handle for the last twenty minutes. The snow is coming down in sheets, blanketing the roads and land around the entire estate. It looks beautiful, like something straight out of a Christmas movie.

The home itself is huge—too big, really. It's made out of the prettiest bright limestone, covered in ivy all the way up to the roof, and the windows, while skinny and set deep into the stone, give the home the coziest feel. Especially now with the whole place decorated for the holidays. The driveway curves in front of the home and is lined with manicured hedges that are lit up with Christmas lights in the setting sun. Gravel and snow crunch under the tires of the Land Rover as Briggs pulls up to the front door. There's smoke pouring out of a few of the chimney stacks that reach high into the air from the third story.

"Mary has your room sorted for you," he says as he puts it in park. "I'll help you get your bags up there." I can feel him staring at me as I soak in my new home. It's daunting, knowing that this whole thing is now mine. The amount of care it takes to run a home like this is no joke. Thank god everyone my aunt hired decided to stay on and help me.

"You alright, my little duck?"

I turn to look at him, a smile forming on my lips at the little nickname he's given me. I'm probably delusional, but I can't help it.

"It's just a lot," I answer honestly. "It's a lot of house, a lot of snow, a lot of *new*. I'm a little intimidated."

"You'll be fine. You've got all of us to help you out. We loved your aunt, and we wouldn't let her only surviving family struggle. Trust me, we've been running this place for so long we could do it with blindfolds on and our hands tied behind our backs."

"I think that would make it a little difficult to keep the hedges cut so evenly."

He graces me with a rough laugh, his eyes crinkling at the sides. I can't help myself—I allow myself for the first time to glance at his left hand. No ring. Is he single?

"Probably." He lays his strong, heavy hand on my shoulder and squeezes. "Let's go inside, get you some food, and get settled in for the evening."

Without waiting for an answer, he turns off the car

and jumps out, letting the cold wind sweep through the cabin. It gets me moving, and I jump out to see Briggs handling all of my luggage himself. I don't even stop to thank him. The snow and wind are so fucking cold that I just let him take over as I run toward the front door.

"I thought I heard that old thing pull up!" Mary yells as she swings the door inward, allowing both of us to practically fall into the warm foyer. Mary is the head housekeeper because yes, this place takes a whole crew to keep running. She's a little older, maybe in her sixties, and her hair is a shining silver that stays braided back out of her face. When I first met her, I instantly felt a connection. Her whole demeanor is soft and welcoming, and she loves this house just as much as everyone has told me my aunt did.

"Hi, Mary!" I wrap my arms around her skinny shoulders, and she holds me tightly. There's a part of her that knows how big and scary this is for me, and I think it's going to be comforting to have a mother figure around the house. She doesn't stay in the home itself; none of the staff do. But there are a few cottages dotted around the property where some of them live, including Mary.

"Don't let all the hot air out, ladies," Briggs says as he squeezes past us. "I'm going to take these up to the room Mary got ready for you, and then I'll head out. Lovely to meet you, Ren." His eyes linger for just a second too long, just long enough for me to notice.

"You drive safely in this snow, you hear?" Mary goes

straight into mothering mode, pulling away from me to give Briggs a hard stare. "And check the generators before you leave?"

Briggs leans in and gives her a quick peck on the cheek, which she accepts with a faint blush. I guess no one is immune to this man and his good looks. My eyes follow him as he walks up the sage-green carpeted stairs, the lighted Christmas swags casting shadows on the wall. Do I let myself take another look at that delicious ass of his? Yes. Yes, I do. And if Mary notices, she doesn't say anything. Instead, she takes my hand and leads me through the formal sitting room, dining room, and into the hallway that leads to the kitchen. It's situated at the back of the home and big enough to cook for hundreds of people.

The whole place has been modernized with indoor plumbing and electricity, but the old-world charm is still everywhere. The fireplaces are huge, taller than me and almost as wide as the walls themselves. Old clay tiles line the floor of the kitchen, there are herbs and flowers hanging in the windows to dry, and the heavy wooden table in the middle of it all has seen better days. But because of all this, the kitchen is one of my favorite rooms. It's like I can feel all the people who have been in here before me: chefs cooking for parties and children running through to grab a snack on their way outside to play.

"I've got your tea on the Aga to keep it warm," Mary tells me, pointing to the range against the far wall. Tea, in

Yorkshire, is what they call dinner, and the Aga is a specific brand of oven that stays warm constantly, heated by oil like the rest of the radiators in the home. The last time I was here, I learned the hot plates on top are great for keeping plates of food warm, as Mary would constantly leave me meals in the evening before she left.

"You didn't have to do that, Mary. I could've fended for myself."

"You could've, but it's nice to have someone around the house again. I'd stay and eat with you," she says as she grabs the plate with a towel and sits it down on the long table, "but I really need to get home before this gets much worse. I didn't think to bring the quad bike over, so I'll be walking."

"Have Briggs take you over there!" I insist. "That's too far for you to walk in this weather, Mary. I'll be worried sick until I hear from you."

"You think I want to get in that rickety old thing?" She looks at me and laughs as she starts to put on her snow boots. She laces them tightly and pulls her thick socks up over her calves. "I'll be safer walking."

"Oh, well, thanks for letting him pick me up in *that old rickety thing*." The chair scrapes against the tile as I pull it out and take a seat. She's made me a single-serving dish of shepherd's pie and what looks to be homemade bread.

Mary laughs and watches me take my first bite. I sink back into my chair with a moan, the mashed potatoes and savory gravy warming me up. "I'll be back tomorrow if I can to check on you and make sure everything is running smoothly. But it's just a house, okay? I know how worried you are. But this place is a house just like all the others you've lived in. Just a bit bigger, is all."

"Yeah, is all," I say around a mouth full of food, rolling my eyes at her.

"Hush." She walks over and leaves a firm kiss on the top of my head. "You know where the thermostats are. They're on low for the unused portions of the house and higher where you'll spend most of your time. If you have *any* questions, my dear, you give me a call. My number is on the fridge."

After she leaves, I continue to eat in silence, the fire crackling to my left. Footsteps fall heavy above my head, and then I hear them move down the hall and the stairs. The front door thuds shut as Briggs leaves, and I'm officially all alone. I've never been one to believe in ghosts, but that was before being left alone in a house that was built over four hundred years ago.

This home creaks and moans in the snowy wind, the floors creak as they settle, and the radiators crack and pop every time they turn on. Everything has an echo, and it's a little unsettling to know there are just so many empty rooms. But the exhaustion and time difference is setting in now that the excitement from the flight and drive is over and my belly is full.

I wash the dishes and set them near the Aga to dry, then make my way back to the front of the house and the grand staircase. I could use the back stairs, but they're skinny and made from worn stone that gives me vertigo every time. So I've resorted to only using the ones built for guests. They're out in the open, relatively level, and aren't hiding spiders.

The room that has become mine is up the stairs and to the right, flanked on both sides by old paintings of my aunt and her beloved whippet. The whole hallway has paintings dating back to the original owners of the home, and while I'm all for displaying art in a home, the eyes kind of creep me out. I have to purposefully keep my eyes on the plush carpet, refusing to watch them watch me as I make my way to my room.

"Oh, thank god," I groan as I enter my room, my bags placed neatly to the side of the door and the bed made and turned down for me. I'm ready to crawl into that sucker and sleep for hours. My pajamas are right on top of my biggest suitcase, along with my basic toiletries. I figured the first thing I would want to do is change into comfortable clothes and brush my teeth. Thank god for past me thinking about future me.

It doesn't take long before I'm crawling between the sheets and curling into the pillows. There's a TV in my room, but I pull out my phone instead, choosing to scroll on social media until my eyes are so heavy I literally can't fight them anymore. I send a quick text to Amie, put my phone on silent, and quickly sink into sleep.

CHAPTER THREE
BRIGGS

THANK Christ I have the keys for the estate. I really thought I'd be able to make it home before the roads got too bad, but this storm isn't letting up. If anything, it's doubled down. The Rover got stuck about a mile down the road, and it was either walk the five miles home or the one mile back to the estate.

I figured Florence would still be awake, but I guess it has almost been an hour since I dropped her off and Mary left. Checking the generators took longer than I thought it would. The snow had piled up around the shed we built to keep them out of the weather, and I had to dig my way in. The house is quiet when I enter; the fireplace in the formal sitting room to my left is the only light and sound.

If I'm being honest with myself, I was kind of hoping she'd still be awake. I wouldn't have hated the chance to get to know her better, watch those pouty lips smile in my direction again. From the moment she walked through the gates into baggage claim, I knew I was in trouble. From her wavy blonde hair to those long, thick legs, this woman was sent to torture me. And then we were in the Rover together, her sweet floral perfume filling the cab. It was a testament to my control not to flirt.

She may be younger than me, but she's my boss, for Christ's sake.

I try to be quiet as I make my way to the back of the house. There's a whole wing that used to be where the servants slept, and we still keep them up for guests or the random tours we sometimes book. So I decide to sleep back there. It's far enough away from Florence that I shouldn't disturb her. She needs her rest after traveling all day. She was tense in the Rover, and not just from the roads. It's like I could smell the panic and anxiety on her. Her foot tapped, and her lip took a beating between her teeth.

Pulling out my phone, I remember that Mary made sure I had Florence's number in case I needed to contact her for anything when I picked her up today. Hopefully, she's put it on silent so that I don't wake her up, but I send her a quick text letting her know that I got stuck and I'm sleeping in one of the downstairs rooms. I don't want to terrify her on her first night.

I strip out of my wet, cold clothes and turn up the radiator on the wall next to the bed. Tossing my jeans onto it to dry, I climb into the cold bed, shivering until the radiator finally clicks and pops, the heat slowly beginning to fill the room. And when I'm comfortable, my mind drifts back to Florence and those plump lips, that perfectly round arse that sat so snugly in her jeans.

My cock comes to life, and I mentally cringe at myself. What a fucking creep. I'm in a room almost directly below my boss, and all I can think about is how she would feel beneath me. And in this moment of weakness, my hand slips beneath my boxers and grips the base of my throbbing cock. I've never been affected by a woman like this before. But every time I close my eyes, all I see is the way her arse moved in those jeans and the way her eyes kept flitting over to me when she thought I wasn't looking.

Using my thumb to collect the precum that's accumulated at my tip, I stroke myself from root to tip. Fuck, I should not be doing this right now. But now that I've started, I can't stop. Her smile and the breathy moans I know she'd make as I tasted her are swimming through my mind. It doesn't take long before I'm coming, spraying over my stomach as I groan into my other hand, trying not to make any noise.

Postorgasmic regret is a real thing, and I instantly feel dirty for what I've done. I use a tissue from the nightstand to clean myself up and then will myself to get some sleep. I'd like to be up and gone before she even checks her phone. The thought of looking her in the eye in the morning after coming to the thought of her is fucking embarrassing.

I WAKE up to a pitch-black room and search for my phone under the pillow. It's not even 2:00 a.m. Stars flash behind my eyelids as I rub my eyes with the heel of my hand, and I roll over to try and get comfortable. These beds are small, and I haven't been this cramped since I was at uni. Right as I'm about to fall back asleep, I hear a loud crash coming from the direction of the kitchen.

Worry sinks into my gut, and I throw the covers back, running out of the room to check on things. Surely it's just Florence. I can't imagine someone has chosen the middle of a blizzard to break into the house. But who knows? I'm not about to just let them ransack the place if it is an intruder.

I round the corner and stride into the kitchen. Florence has her earbuds in, and she's dancing as she digs through the fridge. She's bent over at the waist, white cotton knickers peeking out from under her long T-shirt. Those shapely legs of hers sway her hips side to side, and I have to pull my eyes away from the sight before I get caught perving on my boss.

"It's late," I say as a gentle nudge to let her know I'm here. But her music must be too loud. So I take a few steps closer just as she stands up with her arms full of food. "Hey, it's Briggs."

When I reach out to tap her shoulder, she freaks. Her bloodcurdling scream is loud enough to pop a damn eardrum, and when she turns, all the food drops to the floor. Because she punches me. Right in the fucking eye socket. And then, with a swiftness I didn't expect from her, she knees me right in the fucking crotch.

"Fuck!" I shout, the pain excruciating. I fall to my knees right next to the fridge and then curl up in the fetal position on the floor as I watch her run around the table to turn on the light. It floods the room, making me wince and pull my eyes shut. Fuck, I'm going to vomit.

"Briggs?" she squeals when she finally sees it's me. I peer up at her, and even through the pain, I swear to god I fall in love. She's standing there, butcher knife in hand and hair cascading over her shoulders. Her eyes are wild as she takes in the scene of spilled food and me clutching my balls.

"Yeah. Yeah, it's me," I manage to grunt out as I press my forehead against the cool tile floor. A sick sweat breaks out on my forehead and down my back.

"Oh, god. Oh, Briggs!" I hear the knife get sat down on the counter and then her feet shuffle across the floor before she kneels down next to me. Her soft hand runs up and down my bare arm. Even when I feel like shit, her touch does something to me it shouldn't. "I'm so fucking sorry! I thought you were someone who broke in! Why the fuck are you here?"

"Please, lower your voice. I'm trying to concentrate on not throwing up. Give me a second." I try to push her away. If I do vomit, I don't want her to see it. She swears under her breath, and I hear her stand and walk away.

There's water running, and then she's back, laying a cold, wet cloth on the back of my neck.

I let her take care of me for just a moment. It feels nice to have her fingers running through my hair as she tries to make me feel better. When I take a deep breath and roll over onto my back, she scoots back a few inches, giving me some room.

"I'm so sorry," she whispers, biting her bottom lip.

"Stop that."

"What? Apologizing?"

"No, you can keep doing that," I tease, winking in her direction. The pink on her cheeks deepens. "No, I meant biting your lip. You've been doing it since I picked you up."

"Oh…" Her eyes trail downward from my face, roaming over my half-naked body. Instinctively, I flex, which is such a vain thing to do, but I find I want her to keep looking, and I want her to like what she sees. I'm no gym rat, but I work with my hands on this land every day. It keeps me healthy and strong. Her eyes dance over the tattoos that scrawl over my chest and down my stomach. They dip down into my boxers, and I notice her pupils dilate just slightly at the noticeable bulge.

I clear my throat as I sit up, causing her to snap back to attention. "I did text you," I tell her. "But I'm sorry for scaring you. Rover got stuck about a mile down the road, and figured walking here would be better than walking home."

"Makes sense. I left my phone upstairs, just threw a playlist on and came down. I'm so sorry."

I reach up and gently touch my eyebrow. My fingers come away dotted with blood. "Christ, you really got me, didn't ya?"

"I'm so fucking sorry. Are there ice packs?" She turns and pulls open the bottom door of the freezer, giving me another good look at her panty-covered arse. I have to fight myself not to take her right there, face in the frozen dinners and knickers around her knees. She pulls out a bag of frozen corn and catches me staring at her when she turns around. I don't even try to hide it. I'm sitting here on the floor in my boxer briefs with a blackening eye and sore balls. There's really not much to hide behind.

"Thank you," I say. She gives me a weak smile as she holds the corn against the eye she clobbered. "You have quite the reaction time."

The cutest snort escapes her lips. "Took like three self-defense classes a year ago." She shrugs. "Guess some of it stuck."

"Can't sleep?"

"Not really. The time change has me fucked-up. I was going to make a grilled cheese. Want one?" She gives me another one of her shy smiles. "It's the least I could do."

I should thank her but tell her no. I should get up, walk back to my room, and ice my nuts for the rest of the night and leave her alone. But there's something in her voice that gives me pause. She sounds sad, and maybe she is. It's close to Christmas, and she's in a new country with no friends or family. I'm sure it's a shock to the system. I give her a smile that makes her blush all over again, and I find that I *really* like being able to do that.

"Sure, that'd be great."

"Okay," she says, grinning. "I'll get started."

Chapter Four
Florence

I KNEED Briggs in the balls. And left him with a serious black eye. I feel awful, but you can't go sneaking up on someone like that. Especially when they're in a new house with no pants on.

"Announcing my presence!" I hear him shout as he walks back toward me from the room he's staying in. "I am walking through the hallway! Coming around the corner!"

I laugh, placing the slices of cheese on the bread as the butter sizzles in the pan.

"I am in the doorway!" he announces before taking a step inside. I look at him over my shoulder. He's thrown on his flannel, but it's half-unbuttoned, showing off his strong, tattooed chest, dusted with dark hair. I've never been the girl that likes men shaven. I like them hairy. I want them to look like a man, not a prepubescent boy.

"Thanks for those updates."

His answering smile is enough to drop the panties I'm wearing. No, I didn't go upstairs to put pants on. Should I have? Probably. But I kind of like the way he's been looking at me. I like that maybe I'm the one tempting him.

"So, not a good first night?"

I smile and shake my head. "It was decent until I assaulted you." I flip the sandwiches and then lean against the counter, crossing my arms, watching him watch me. Those pretty dark eyes of his roam my body openly, like he wants me to see he's interested—that he likes what he sees. It makes my hair stand on end, and my stomach swoops and flutters. "Didn't think those classes really stuck. Guess they did."

"Guess so," he says, finally meeting my eyes again. "You have quite the right hook."

I shrug, turning my attention back to the sandwiches. The heat from the Aga warms my bare legs almost as much as his gaze does. I can feel it on me like a physical touch, and it blurs the lines that should be between us. Technically, I'm his boss. I don't really like that term, but it is what it is. Even though he's clearly a good decade older than me, I inherited the house, and he works at it. Getting involved would probably not be the best idea.

He walks over beside me, grabbing a couple of plates from the cabinet and setting them on the counter. Using the spatula, I take the sandwiches out of the pan and place them on the plates. I have to admit, these look good. They're golden brown, and the thick-cut cheddar cheese is melting over the crust of the bread. Using the butter knife, I cut mine in half, diagonally through the center.

"Diagonal?" he asks, his one eyebrow rising.

"There is no other way."

He narrows his eyes, watching me as he cuts his right down the center.

I gasp. "You monster."

He takes a bite and winks, making a goofy smile break out across my face. I look away, hiding the fact that this man can affect me so much. I take a bite of my own, moaning at how good the buttery bread and melted cheese taste together.

"What is it about late-night food that tastes so much better?" I ask, glancing back over in his direction. But he isn't paying attention. No, his eyes are locked on my lips. "What?" I ask, wiping at my mouth. "Do I have cheese stuck to my mouth?"

He makes a strangled noise and shakes his head, setting the plate back down on the counter before taking a step in my direction. I'm frozen on the spot, not sure where he's taking this. There's a very large part of me that wants him to take me right here on this counter. I'm not sure if it's the jet lag or the late-night grilled cheese endorphins, but this man has my toes curling against the tile just from *looking* at me.

"That little noise you made..." he starts, his voice barely above a whisper. He slowly closes the distance between us completely, and that masculine scent of his fills my senses and knocks me off-balance. His calloused hands cautiously take hold of my face, jaw, and throat, his thumbs softly moving back and forth over my cheeks. I'm tall for a woman, but Briggs is still taller, forcing my head to fall back to look at him.

We share a breath, our gazes flicking back and forth between eyes and lips. There's a hint of a smile on those sexy lips of his, the ghost of a dimple peeking out from under his scruff. When I lick my lips, he zeroes in on them, no longer able to hold my gaze. I let myself touch him then, my fingertips sliding along the band of his boxer briefs and then settling under his shirt on the soft skin of his hips.

"I probably shouldn't be doing this," he murmurs, his eyes flicking to mine for the briefest second before going back to my mouth.

"Probably not," I agree, my voice rough from nerves.

A quick, deep chuckle rumbles through his chest. "I don't think I can stop myself, though," he admits. "Not unless you want me to."

My fingertips dig into his sides, pulling him even closer to me, forcing him to brush up against my body. He's warm and hard all over, his body finely tuned from all those years of hard work with his hands. Oh, god. I bet he's so fucking good with his hands. My thighs clench at the thought.

"Do I look like I want you to stop?"

He hesitates, just slightly, his head bobbing once before slowly descending to meet mine. His hands stay cupped around my face, pulling me to meet him halfway. The kiss is gentle at first, slow and teasing, testing the waters. His lips are soft against my own, barely opening as he leaves sweet pecks from one corner to the other, like he's cherishing every little second. I've never been kissed like this, like it matters, like *I* matter.

Pulling back, he looks at me for a second, making sure I really want this. And, god help me, I do. I really, really do. The nod I give him is small, almost imperceptible. But he sees it, and he seizes the opportunity. This time when he kisses me, he *really* kisses me. His hands tighten their grip, one sliding to rest at the back of my neck and the other continuing to hold me fast against his mouth.

When I feel his tongue slide against the seam of my lips, I part them and let him in. He tastes like buttery bread as his tongue slides over mine. The rough stubble rubs deliciously over my mouth and chin, and I finally let my fingers work at the buttons of his flannel, exposing his torso. My hands roam over his stomach and chest. His abs flex under my palms; the hair over his pecs is soft. I love the way he almost purrs against me, a low growl rolling through him and vibrating into me.

With quick movements and never lifting his mouth from my own, he shucks his shirt off and lets it land on the tile beneath us. Then, he's grabbing my ass and hoisting me up against him, and my legs immediately wrap around his hips before he guides me down onto the wooden table in the center of the room. His body hovers over me, his lips, teeth, and tongue still ravaging my mouth.

"Briggs," I breathe against him as he abandons my mouth for my jaw and throat. He works his way down, licking and sucking as he goes. My panties are soaked, and my toes are curled. My body feels like it's on fire, too hot to have this shirt on any longer.

"Tell me to stop." He breaks, his forehead resting just below my collarbone while his fingers play with the hem of my shirt. "Tell me to stop, and I'll stop, Ren."

Those dark eyes look up at me, his mouth swollen and red from our impassioned kissing. His eyelashes are long and dark. *Why do men always have the prettiest fucking eyelashes?* I run my hands through his hair, tousling it into messy waves. I shake my head back and forth, and that's enough for him. I lift my hips, and he pushes my shirt up and over my hips and stomach, exposing my skin to the slight chill in the room.

My nipples pebble as he continues pushing upward before helping me lift it off completely. The way he looks down at me has my body heating to an uncomfortable level. His eyes eat me up while his fingers trace lines from my collarbone to between my breasts, then over my navel and down to the band of my cotton underwear. Had I known this was a possibility, I would've worn something a little more sexy than granny panties.

"God, you're sexy," he says, his eyes flashing back up to mine. His arms wrap around my thighs, and he tugs me roughly to the edge of the table so that I'm flush with his hips. I love the way he can manhandle me and the way his fingers curl into my flesh, dimpling my skin with the effort. "And these little white knickers?" he practically growls, running a single digit over my mound and between my thighs. The sensation causes my back to arch and a pained moan to escape my lips. I need more than what he's giving me. I need him to fucking *touch* me.

"Briggs," I groan, my hips lifting to find more friction. "Please."

"Fuck, I love it when you beg. You look so pretty beneath me, squirming and needy." His pupils are blown, and his hands grab hold of my hips as he leans forward slightly. It's just enough to make contact with my clit, his rock-hard cock pressing firmly against it.

Fuck. I am doomed. I'd do just about anything to make him touch me right now. When I reach down and grab hold of his forearms—the easiest thing for me to reach—I dig my nails in and use them as leverage to grind my pussy against his boxer-clad cock. He's so hard, and I can see where he's dripping precum, turned on and already wet for me.

Briggs leans forward again, one of his hands wrapping around my throat. He holds it snugly but doesn't squeeze. I like the way it feels, safe and held in place against a man who clearly wants me. His thumb runs along my jaw and then slips between my lips, where I suck it hard into my mouth.

The darkest chuckle rolls through him as he smirks at my brazenness.

"I bet you will be the best girl for me," he says, his eyes locked onto mine. "Won't you, Ren?"

CHAPTER FIVE
BRIGGS

OH, fuck. What am I doing right now? Why have I let it go this far?

I look down at Ren, her body on display for me like a damn buffet, and I'm starving. I'm ready to taste every single part of her. Her teeth graze over the knuckle of my thumb, and my hips flex and push against her. Those golden-hazel eyes of hers roll into the back of her head from the friction, and I can't think of a more beautiful sight.

Running my hands over her body, her soft skin pebbling beneath, I notice just how soft she is. Not only her skin but the contours of her shape, the way her hips flare and her stomach curves slightly under her navel. The heaviness of her breasts causes them to lean slightly to either side of her rib cage, and I take them both in my palms before rolling her pink nipples between my fingers. She's so responsive, giving me whimpers, gasps, and moans with every touch.

When I kneel on the cold tile floor, her hands leave my hair and instead take purchase above her head to hold on to the edge of the table. Her lungs expand with her deep breathing, and she watches my movements closely, her lids heavy and pupils wide with lust.

I never thought I'd be here, between this gorgeous woman's thighs in the middle of the night on a kitchen table. Although, I'm not complaining. I've been fighting for dominance with my dick ever since I saw her walk through customs and right up to me with a cautious smile. And now here she is, laid almost bare in front of me, begging me to touch her.

How the hell did a man like me get so lucky?

She lifts her hips as I tug gently on her panties, pulling them over her thighs and down her calves, tossing them to the side. When I guide her feet back to the edge of the table, she pushes her knees together, essentially hiding exactly what I want.

"Spread these for me, princess," I tell her, kissing her shin as I softly urge her to reposition her legs. She hesitates but does as I say, pushing her feet a little wider and letting her knees open. "Jesus Christ," I murmur under my breath when I finally get to see her glistening pink pussy.

"What?" she asks, her voice nervous as she sits up on her elbows. Worry swims over her features, and I'm eager to put them to rest.

"You're just so fucking perfect." I bite the inside of her thigh and then lick and suck on the spot. She watches, still propped up on her arms. I kiss my way down her thigh, holding her gaze the entire time until I'm finally at the apex of her thighs. "I'm going to taste you, Ren," I tell her, kissing just about where she wants me most. "And I want to hear all those sweet little moans and whimpers. I don't want you to hold back. You tell me exactly what you want and what you need, and I'll give it to you."

She bites her plump lower lip and nods, still watching me so intently. My cock is dripping into my boxers, begging to be released. But I ignore it because all I need right now is to taste her—to feel her come apart on my tongue. I finally drop my eyes down to her cunt, use my thumbs to spread her open for me, and then lick her from bottom to top, her sweet and musky flavor exploding on my tongue.

A small whimper escapes those pouty lips when I reach her clit and circle it slowly, over and over again. My thumbs keep her spread for me, teasing the nerves along her opening while my lips close over her clit and suck. She drops back on the table then, the hard *thunk* echoing through the room before her moans drown it out. Her hips begin to buck and roll, and I wrap an arm around them to hold her in place while my other hand teases her opening.

I wet one finger, sliding it through her folds as I

continue working on her clit, and then slowly slip it inside before curling it to search for that sweet spot.

"Briggs!" She practically screams when I find it, and I grin against her wetness as I massage her G-spot. Fuck, she's tight. And her Kegels are squeezing the life out of my finger, sending signals down to my cock that I struggle to ignore. There's almost nothing I want more than to sink inside of her wet heat, but her pleasure comes first, and I'll be damned if she gets my cock before she gets an orgasm.

I eat her like a starving man gone mad, adding another finger while I lick, suck, and nibble every part of her I can get to. She moans above me, one hand playing with her nipples while the other arm is flung over her face, like the pleasure is just too good to handle.

"Briggs, I'm gonna come."

I don't answer, just keep going. I keep my rhythm steady, my movements the same. There's no way I'm changing a single thing when she's this close to the finish line. Her stomach heaves with her breath, and her fingers roughly pull her left nipple so hard it's lifting her breast. She's beautiful—perfect. Everything about her. Her taste, her moans, those hazel eyes, and plush lips. There's not a single thing to find fault with.

And when she eventually comes, her back arches, and her mouth drops open. My name is whispered on her lips over and over again as the orgasm wracks through her body. The muscles deep inside of her clench and pulse against my fingers, and I slow my movements, letting her come down before she gets over-stimulated.

"Holy shit," she swears, breathing heavily as I slip my fingers free of her cunt and stand back up to my full height. She watches me as I lick my fingers and lips, then wipe her juices from my chin. I give the side of her arse a little smack, making a sweet smile break out across her face as she giggles. "I really hope you have more in you," she continues. "Because I can't wait to see what else you can do."

I laugh and smack her arse again, loving the way her flesh jiggles when I do so. I've never been a man that likes his woman to be skin and bones, instead favoring women like Ren with sexy-as-fuck curves and an arse big enough to hold on to. She watches me as I take off the last piece of clothing between us, my cock springing free as the boxers drop to the floor. Her eyes widen as it bobs between us, eager to be deep inside that sweet little pussy of hers.

Gripping the base, I press the tip against her swollen clit, running it up and down her slit to soak myself with her release. My cock is thick and long, with a slight upward curve at the end. There have been some women who have struggled to take all of me, and while Ren is tight, I know she's my woman. And she will be able to take all of me like the good fucking girl she is.

"Tell me now, princess," I growl, taking hold of her throat with my free hand to grab her attention. "Tell me now if I need to stop because I don't have a condom, and

I'm clean, but if you want one, I'll stop. I need you to tell me now, though. Because I'm losing control."

"No, it's okay," she says with urgency. "I'm clean. Practically celibate and on the pill. Just fuck me. Please, Briggs." Her hand shoots out and takes control of my cock, giving it a few rough strokes as she lines us up together. Her eyes meet mine, and I am fucking gone. "Please," she begs one more time.

CHAPTER SIX
FLORENCE

IN ONE SWIFT THRUST, Briggs bottoms out inside of me. The stretch is intense, and he fills me so incredibly that I lose my breath and arch my back off the table. Briggs holds me against him, one hand on my hips and his other arm wrapped underneath my lower back. He slowly lifts me so that we're face-to-face, my legs wrapped around his hips and our mouths hovering just an inch away from each other.

This new position lets me grind against him, giving my clit some much-needed friction. I love the way his hands are just all over me, from my hips to my breast to my back. They hold me close and tangle in my hair, tugging my head back to expose my neck to his mouth. He licks, sucks, and bites all while his scruff scratches. I'm a panting mess, moaning and whimpering with each thrust he gives me.

Every single one is deep, hitting a spot inside of me

that no one has ever hit before. It's a new kind of pleasure, one that builds slowly but no less intense. It builds and builds until I feel like I'm going to break.

"That's it, princess," he whispers in my ear before biting the shell. "I can feel you're so close. You want to come for me?"

I make a soft, plaintive sound, not able to give him a clear answer because the pleasure is just too overwhelming. And knowing that this rough and handsome man in front of me is the one doing it just skyrockets everything higher. I've never been so attracted to someone right off the bat like this, and it's kind of sending me for a loop. Not only that, but I've never been one to have a one-night stand. Not that I judge those who do, but it's just not me. Normally, I need an emotional connection, not just physical attraction.

But with Briggs, that is all off the table. Or…on it, I guess.

"Answer me, Ren," he says in between kisses. "I want to hear you say it."

I growl in frustration, the bratty side of me coming out. "Yes," I tell him with as much attitude as I can muster in the moment. "Yes, I want to come, Briggs."

Another dark laugh rumbles through him. I hate how much I like them—how much I like *him*. "Good girl. I knew you'd be so good for me."

His pace picks up as his fingers slip between us, finding my clit and teasing it with soft, consistent circles. It doesn't take long before the pleasure building low in my belly explodes, stealing my breath as he continues to kiss me through it. My head falls back, and he abandons my mouth, instead resting his head on my shoulder. I throw my arms around his neck and hold on as he plows into me, his hands digging into my hips as he pulls and pushes me against him in time with his thrusts.

The table creaks and moans beneath us, and my ass burns from chafing against the rough wood. He whispers my name over and over again, along with some obscenities for flavor, as he comes. His mouth finds mine again while his hands move to hold my face. I can taste myself still on his tongue as it swipes against my own, and when we both finally come down, we both just look at each other.

"All I wanted was a grilled cheese."

He throws his head back in laughter, gives me a soft smack on my ass, and then lifts me off the table. "Let's go get cleaned up, and then we can finish the sandwiches." And while he's still inside of me, he carries me through the large home—*my* large home—and up the stairs to the bedroom that is now mine.

There's a bathroom that's attached with a large walk-in shower. He lets us slip apart as he sets me back on my feet before entering the shower. It's huge, with frosted glass that blocks his view while he turns on the water.

"Do your business," he says, peeking around the corner and pointing to the toilet. "Have a piss to keep yourself healthy, and then get your arse in here with me so that I can take care of you."

"You want me to pee? Right here?" My eyes are wide as he looks at me, confused.

"What, you going to go in here? You into piss play?" he asks, my face heating from the insinuation. "Because if you are, I'm down, I guess. But I'd like to talk through it first. Boundaries are healthy."

That stupid mischievous grin is back, and I want so badly to playfully smack it off his face. "No, I am *not* into piss play."

"Not that there's anything wrong with that!" he calls out as he dips back inside the shower. The steam is fogging up the glass even more, and I realize that this man has no shame or embarrassment. He really is expecting me to just sit my ass down and pee with him right there.

So instead of fighting it, *whatever*, I flip the switch on the wall that turns on the exhaust fan and then do my business while he sings some unknown song way off tune. When I finally join him, he grins and grabs my hand, tugging me toward him into the hot water. His hands smooth back my hair as he spins us and puts me under the water, and then he kisses me again and again and again…

"EVER BEEN MARRIED?"

He takes a sip of his wine and grins at me over the rim. "Oh, we're diving into the hard questions now?"

"I don't know," I say, nudging him with my foot. "Is that a hard one?"

After our shower, we made new sandwiches, and he poured us some wine, and now we're in the den with the fire lit. The den is different from the rest of the home. It's cozy, with a large, brown leather sectional that has the deepest seats I've ever seen in my life and soft blankets thrown everywhere. There's a large TV above the fireplace and thick, lush rugs to cover the worn flooring.

"I was engaged once," he admits, watching me for my reaction. I don't give him one. I don't care if he's been married eight times—okay, well, maybe eight is pushing it—I just want to know about *him*. "We were young. She got pregnant, and I did what I thought I was supposed to do. I proposed, we planned, and then four months in, she lost the baby."

"Oh, Briggs." I sit up and reach over to touch his arm. "I'm so sorry." I've never wanted kids, but that doesn't mean I can empathize with someone who has lost one. I can't imagine the pain of losing something you wanted so, so much.

"It was hard at first," he admits, giving me a sad smile. "But, I have to admit, I never saw myself as Dad. I don't think I was born with that fatherly gene. Don't get me wrong, I would've loved that kid and given them anything they wanted in life. But it wasn't something I dreamed of, ya know?"

I nod, giving him a light squeeze.

"Anyway, without the baby, we drifted apart...

quickly. She came to me one evening and told me she wanted to part ways. I wasn't against it, so we parted amicably. Haven't gotten that close since." He finishes his wine and grabs the bottle. "Not for lack of trying, though," he says with a laugh. "I may not want kids, but that doesn't mean I don't want a family. A wife and a dog —or seven—has been the dream."

"Or seven?" I laugh, but it sounds exactly like what I've wanted.

"I'm a sucker for those rescues." He shrugs. "What about you? You want a husband and kids?"

"A husband, sure. Kids? Not really." I drink my own wine, trying to give myself some liquid courage. I've only known this man for twelve hours, but I want him to know we want the same things, that maybe we could keep this thing going and see where we end up. Which, yes, sounds insane. But I tend to be the person who falls first and falls the fastest. It's a personality trait I've worked hard on but clearly still haven't overcome. "Same as you; I don't really feel like I was born with that mothering gene."

He moves on the couch, spinning around and lying down so that his head rests on my lap. His wine sloshes a bit in his glass, but he manages to set it down on the floor without spilling a drop. Not being able to stop myself, I run my hands through his slightly damp hair. His eyes close for a second before he looks back up at me.

"I feel I should apologize," he says, grinning. "For scaring you, for pushing myself on you afterwards."

My cheeks flame, and I take another sip for bravery. "Don't be," I tell him. "Clearly, I wanted it, too."

He grabs my arm, kisses the inside of my wrist, and then drapes it over his chest. "I would like to be honest with you for a minute, if that's okay."

"Always," I answer, setting my wine down on the table behind me so that I can give him my full attention.

"Being forty-five, I've kind of given up on the whole *finding someone* thing. It feels like I'm too old now." My stomach drops, and I can't help but feel a little disappointment. "But, I dunno, you walked through those doors at baggage claim, and I—"

"Fell in love with me immediately, right?" I tease. "It's to be expected."

The joke worked, diffusing some of the tension that had built up between us. "Exactly," he says, grinning up at me. "Indeed, I did know I was done for when I saw you. You were red and flustered, and I botched it, barely being able to get a word out."

My insides are swirling with unbridled *glee*. I'm not kidding, I feel like I'm floating on cloud-fucking-nine right now. Biting the inside of my lip to keep myself from grinning like a fool, I meet his eyes and nod.

"I thought you were pretty good-looking, too," I admit.

"Even though I'm old enough to be your dad?"

I guffaw. "My dad?" I practically squeal. "How young do you think I am? You'd have had to have me at like seventeen! Which, I guess, now that I'm saying it out loud, is totally plausible, but you are not too old for me." I grab my wine again and drink the rest of it, downing half a glass even though it brutally burns the entire way down.

Word vomit.

I cringe at how desperate or crazy I may have just seemed. But when I look back down at him, he's smiling, his fingers tracing soft lines up and down my arm. His eyes look heavy, and I realize he's been up with me all night with hardly any sleep.

The sun is starting to come up, the snow making it seem brighter than it really is. When I pull myself away from his eyes to look out the back window, I see the snow is still coming down. And it even looks like it's accumulated up past the window sill. Maybe we'll be snowed in. Maybe we'll have a few days together to figure out if we want to keep this going—if this can work. In our own little bubble of Christmas and snow.

"Still snowing," I say softly before looking back down at him. His eyes are closed, the ghost of a smile on his lips and his hands still holding on to my arm. Taking a deep breath, I try to settle the butterflies that haven't stopped for hours now. I let my head drop back to the soft cushions of the couch and close my eyes.

Chapter Seven
Florence

I JOLT AWAKE, my body violently jumping.

"What? Huh?" Briggs falls off the couch, sending his glass of wine spilling and rolling—thankfully—onto the floor instead of the rug. "Bollocks!"

I laugh while he rushes to pick up the glass, his hair a mess and eyes still heavy with sleep.

"It's okay, Briggs," I tell him, stretching as I move to get off the couch. "It's just a floor. I'll get a rag."

"It's okay. I'll get it," he says, smiling and leaning over to kiss me softly on the lips. Then my nose. And then my forehead.

He jogs off, and I smile as I watch him go. That ass in those boxer briefs should come with a warning. I stand, avoiding the spilled wine, and tidy up our blankets, plates, and glassware. I'm just throwing a folded blanket onto the back of the sectional when he comes walking back in, rag in hand and cheeks red. When he catches my eye, he looks shy.

"What's wrong?"

He shrugs and presents me with a piece of lined yellow paper. "I hope—I dunno. I just…I hope this doesn't upset you."

I can feel my brows knit together as he starts cleaning, and I start reading.

Trudged over early this morning when there was a break in the snow. Figured you'd need some help checking the generators or stirring the fires. Looks like someone else beat me to it ;) Have fun, be safe. I'll be back over once the storm clears. — Mary

"Oh…my god."

"Yeah," he grunts from the floor. "Whoops."

I look out the window, seeing the snow has not let up. It's piled up past the windowsill now. "How did she even get over here?" I ask, probably sounding a bit more hysterical than I mean to.

"Mary takes her job very seriously." His tone is still joking, but he refuses to look at me. Instead, he wipes the same spot on the floor over and over again. There's no wine left, and there's no stain. It's like he's too, what? Ashamed? Embarrassed? "She would get here if the snow was ten feet high just to make sure this place was still standing."

"I—" I start, but can't really get the words out. I'm trying my hardest not to laugh. Because this is most certainly something that would happen to me. It's just my luck that on my first day as *woman of the house*, or whatever, I would be caught half-naked with an employee. Christ. "I'm so sorry," I get out before I snort, and my hand flies to my mouth to cover up the embarrassment.

He looks up, humor twinkling in those dark eyes. "You just snorted."

"Shut up."

Briggs laughs, one strong cackle of a laugh as he stands and tosses the stained-purple rag onto the hearth. "Did you just tell me to shut up, little duck?"

I narrow my eyes at him, a flirty reproach that he sees right through. Or ignores. "You should never point out a lady's flaws," I scold.

He hums, closing the distance between us, taking my face in his hands. My god, this man is good. Every time he's about to kiss me, he holds me so close, so carefully. His palms are warm, and one of his thumbs traces my bottom lip.

"Shall I point out your assets instead?" His eyebrow does a perfect arch, melting my panties all over again. "Like how you give me the sweetest little moans when I'm inside of you?"

I blush…furiously.

"Or how these cute, round cheeks blush so prettily when you're embarrassed?"

I roll my eyes.

"How about how kind you are to the people who work here?" he asks, continuing like he's not flustering the fuck out of me. "I heard all about you after you came to visit that first time. *What a sweet girl*, they all said. *So kind, so interested in everything we do. She's going to be great*." He pauses, kissing the tip of my nose. "For an American, anyway."

I scoff and push on his chest, but he grabs me, laughing as he pulls me flush against him. "Hush, pretty girl. You're perfect, even with that Yank accent of yours. I actually find it endearing."

"Oh, do you?" I ask, my voice laced with sarcasm. I wish I could tease him about his accent, but there's no way I could be convincing. Because it's the single most sexy thing I've ever heard. Especially when filthy things are being said.

"I do," he says, nodding and playing with the ends of my hair. "And your eyes?" he asks, locking his gaze with my own. "Green in the sunlight and honey-colored in the firelight." He makes a desperate little noise. "Beautiful."

He leans in, glancing his lips against my own. I can feel myself falling into him, our breaths mixing as our mouths barely touch. Briggs holds me up, supports my weight against his own. I love how tall he is. It's rare that I get to be so dwarfed by a man, and I'm finding it intoxicating.

"Don't you want to say anything nice about me?"

I break out in laughter, my head falling back. But he just smiles and catches it, pulling my mouth immediately back to his, where he kisses me like his life damn near depends on it. His tongue dives in, exploring and savoring. The feeling of his hands holding me to him just sets my nerves on fire.

"So you aren't worried about her knowing?" he asks, his voice rough from the kiss. His eyes are wary, looking at me like I might give him the news he doesn't want to hear.

But I shake my head back and forth slowly. "I'm not." I run my hands over the strong muscles of his back. "Are you?"

"I thought I would be," he admits. "Last night, before *everything*." His chuckle is soft and sweet. "I was worried I was overstepping, that I should keep my goddamn dick in my trousers. But then you were in the kitchen, swinging your hips with those white cotton knickers peeking out beneath your shirt." He bites his lip and grins. "Nothing could've prepared me for that."

Without warning, he grabs my hand and pushes me away before spinning me under his arm and pulling my back into his chest. He wraps me up, one hand holding mine against my chest and the other resting gently against my stomach. His hips start to sway to invisible music, and I let my head fall back onto his shoulder. A soft kiss is pressed to my temple, that stubble tickling my cheek.

"Will you let me stay?" he asks, his lips pressed against my ear and then farther down to my neck. "We could watch movies and get to know each other. I'll cook for you, and you can just sit there and look pretty for me."

Where the hell did this man come from?

I nod, turning my head a bit so that I can see his handsome face. His age shows in some spots: the faint wrinkles in the corners of his eyes and the salt that's starting to show around his temples. But he's gorgeous. Breathtaking, really.

"I don't think it would be good for my image to shove you back out into the snow." I grin up at him. "The others would gossip."

He spins me back out and then pulls me swiftly back in, this time facing him. His eyes are full of mirth at my remark, but then everything turns a little more serious. I think we both realize how much we want this and how perfect this could be. It's nice to see yourself and your wants mirrored in someone else.

We dance like this for a while, him humming off-key and me laughing when he *really* gets it wrong. After a while, he pulls me in the direction of the couch, our bodies spinning until finally he sits and tugs me down on top of him. I straddle him, settling easily into his body. It's intimate, and I feel him harden beneath me.

He groans and runs his fingers through my hair. I love how obsessed he seems to be with it, always twirling or touching it. "Part of me wishes I had taken it slower with you," he tells me. Quietly, like it's a secret.

"Why?" My own fingers play with his hair and then settle where his neck meets his shoulders.

"Because I don't want you to think that's the kind of man I am. I'm not the man who sleeps with women on the first date. I'm not a man who only wants sex." He takes a deep breath, letting out a sigh filled with worry. "Not with you, Florence."

I nod, massaging the knots in his shoulders. "I've always been the girl that gets too attached." I laugh at myself. "I always had a crush, always chasing a boy. I don't know what makes me fall first and fast, but that's just who I am. I've learned to accept it about myself as I've grown. So to hear that you want to accept that we have something here, to explore it and try, it's a type of validation I don't think I've ever received."

I should be embarrassed. There's a part of my brain that is currently screaming at me to shut up. But Briggs looks at me like I have his undivided attention, like he's really interested in what I'm saying. Like he *understands*.

"Not that I want to run off and get married or anything," I tease.

"You sure?" he asks, his eyes lighting up playfully. "I have a friend that would do it in a heartbeat."

I shove him playfully. "I'm sure. I'd like to get to know you a little better first, I think."

"Well," he says, shrugging. "I guess I can get on board with that. But I am sorry for one thing."

"Yeah?" I ask, my face showing my confusion.

"I didn't get you anything for Christmas."

I laugh, and he tackles me back onto the couch, kissing me senseless. And I think this might just be the gift I needed.

CHAPTER EIGHT
BRIGGS

THE REST of our day was spent checking on things around the house. I told her I would do it, but she was eager to learn, so she followed me around and helped where she could. The generators are still good to go, filled with petrol and kept dry out in the shed. Getting out there was an *experience*. We opened the door to a wall of snow, and I realized quickly that I am not in as good of shape as I thought.

Ren helped me carry firewood and clean the fireboxes and hearths, and luckily, she found some old men's clothes hiding away in one of the rooms. The sweatpants are a little on the small side, but it's better than wearing the same boxers for days on end. She was dressed in these tight, silky-looking leggings, with tall, fluffy socks and a hoodie. Her hair was tied up in a knot of waves, exposing her long neck to my wandering eyes. It's been a testament to my self-control that I haven't taken her in one of the many rooms.

More than a few times, she looked over at me, giving me a look that was pure heat. The tension between us is insane. I never thought I would feel something like this, especially so quickly. I don't know if it's the low lighting of the Christmas decorations, painting everything in a warm, romantic glow, or if it's just *us*. Just *her*.

She's upstairs taking a bath and soaking her sore muscles. Between the rough shagging I gave her last night and the manual labor she insisted she do today, I think she's a little exhausted. Which is fine with me. It gives me time to clean up the kitchen and cook her a meal. I can't really take her on a date since we're stuck here until the plows can make it to us, and with the Christmas holidays happening for the next three days, I don't think that'll be happening anytime soon.

There are lighted swags on both of the windows in the kitchen and a warmly lit tree in the corner. I rummaged around in the decorations that Mary left lying out and found a plaid tablecloth and some old candles. They're not the prettiest, but they'll do. The table has also been disinfected since our little romp, and the rolls in the oven are filling the room with the scent of garlic.

I decided to make her some pasta. She is a carbs girl, and I love that about her. Because with all the labor I do on a daily basis, I tend to eat my body weight in carbs. So I threw together a little cheese tortellini with a creamy tomato sauce and found Mary's recipe for her famous garlic bread knots.

Her footsteps fall on the stairs, and I'm eager to see what she's decided to wear. I told her I'd have a surprise for her once she was ready and asked her to wear her nicest outfit she brought. While I don't have many options, I did wash *my* clothes, buttoning the flannel up to the top for a bit more formality, and hoped that pairing it with my jeans would look good enough.

"Should I announce myself?" she calls out as I hear her shoes click against the wood floor in the hallway.

I smile as I stir the sauce. "Probably best!" I shout back. "I have an unblemished record of never hitting a woman. Would like to keep it that way!"

"So? How do I look?" she asks when closer, her voice low and sweet.

When I turn around to look at her, I can feel the smile on my face drop. Because *fuck me*, this woman is exquisite. The dress she's put on is a dark red velvet, and it hugs every single one of her curves. Her sleeves are long, and the neckline is dangerously low. She does a spin, causing the bottom to flare out and up, almost giving me a glimpse of her luscious arse. Her hair hangs around her shoulders in waves, framing her round cheeks and hazel eyes.

"Wow." It's all I can manage. I've thought she was stunning every step of the way, from her being travel-tired to middle-of-the-night sex to waking up on the sofa with me. She's been stunning…breathtaking, even. But now? Good god. She radiates in the low, cozy light from the Christmas tree and candles.

Her eyes move from my stunned face to the table, where I've set up our nice plates, the candles, and the on-theme tablecloth. In a split second, her eyes are watery, and her hand goes to her mouth.

"I wanted to do something nice for you," I tell her, walking over to where she stands in the doorway. She has heels on, making her just as tall as I am, and I love that I now have even easier access to her mouth. Her eyes struggle to meet mine, and I see a few tears escape. "Hey," I whisper, taking her in my arms and kissing her on the cheek. "What's wrong?"

"This is really nice," she whispers, finally able to look me in the eye. She wipes away the tears and then rolls her eyes to hide the emotions rolling through her. "No one has ever really done this for me. And while I knew you were down here doing something, I didn't think it would be…this."

I take the opportunity to kiss her, my hands moving straight to the soft curls in her hair. Nothing makes me happier than this. Just to hold her and taste her, it's fucking ruining me in the best way.

"Come, come." I break the kiss, grabbing her hand and leading her over to the table. Pulling out one of the chairs, I gesture with an exaggerated bow that she should sit. "For you, my lady," I say in the poshest voice I can manage. I grew up in the moors, so my accent is thick and country. The Queen's English feels like a foreign language on my tongue.

But Ren just laughs, curtsies, and mimics the accent as well. "Why, thank you. What a gentleman."

"Okay, maybe don't try that again," I tease, poking fun at her failed attempt at the accent. Mine was bad, but hers? *Woof.*

She gives me a playful smack on the hip and then leans back, picking up the glass of wine I poured for her a few minutes ago. Her pouty lips take a sip, and I have to fight the urge to groan. I've yet to see what those lips look like wrapped around my cock, and I'm desperate to experience it.

"What's on the menu, chef?" she asks as I pull the garlic knots out of the oven. They're a perfect golden brown, and I grab the melted butter to pour over them while they're still hot.

"Well, I know you mentioned liking a good pasta dish, so I made you a cheese tortellini with a tomato sauce from scratch. And I was lucky enough to find Mary's garlic knots recipe, so I threw those together as well."

"It smells amazing. My stomach was growling while I was in the bath." She laughs, and the sound makes my stomach flip. Christ, when did I turn into a teenage boy with a crush?

"Lucky you," I say, shoving the nerves down deep as I load up our plates with food. "It's ready now."

Once the plates are on the table, she tugs me down

for a kiss and whispers, "Thank you," against my mouth. Our eyes lock, and I swear everything pauses for a second. *What a sap*, I think to myself. But honestly, it's okay with me. This woman deserves a man who will be a sap for her, cook her food, and dote on her. And I'll be damned if it'll be any man but myself.

OUR PLATES ARE EMPTY, the sun has fully set, and her cheeks are pink from the wine. She looks gorgeous sitting there with her legs crossed and a glass of wine in her hand. Ren smiles at me over her glass before finishing what's there. I think we're both thinking about what happened right here less than twenty-four hours ago. I'll never be able to look at this table again.

Shit, maybe we should replace it. Thinking about all of my coworkers eating at the table I fucked their boss on gives me a not-so-great feeling.

"Do you have any Christmas traditions?" she asks, her voice pulling me out of my thoughts.

"Actually, yes. Good thing you brought that up." I laugh. "I normally go to my sister's. I'll have to call her to let her know I won't be there."

"I'm just now realizing how little I know about you," she says, giggling. "Tell me about your family. Is she your only sister? What about your parents?"

"Seeing as I met you yesterday, I don't think I should expect you to know my family tree." I grin in her direction before pulling her chair closer to me. Grabbing her calf, I place her right foot on my lap and work on the small buckle at her ankle. "Tess is my only sibling. She's been married for about ten years now. Dom is a great guy, and they have two kids together: Maya and Oliver."

Her head falls back when I begin to massage her foot and ankle, one of those sensual little moans escaping her lips. "That feels so good. I'm rethinking the marriage proposal."

I wink at her. "Don't tempt me, little duck."

Smiling and rolling her eyes, she continues. "Maya and Oliver." Her lips form a cute little pout. "What cute names."

"Cute, but mischievous little buggers. They're twins," I tell her, widening my eyes and shaking my head. "I think Dom almost shit himself with that ultrasound."

"God," she groans, making a strained face. "Twins are what nightmares are made of. I mean, not that your niece and nephew are nightmares." Her face scrunches up.

"No offense taken," I tell her sincerely. "Trust me, they're the stuff of my nightmares as well. Love them to pieces, but love even more that I can give them back at the end of the day." I finish my own glass before continuing. "As far as our parents go, they passed away in a car accident a few years back. Drunk driver."

"Oh, Briggs." Her eyes instantly lose all their humor, and she reaches out to grab my hand. "I'm so sorry."

"Still hurts sometimes, but I'm a firm believer there's something there when we go. Not *Heaven*, necessarily. But something. And I figure they're looking down on me right now, hoping I don't fuck this"—I gesture between us—"up."

Her smile returns, and it takes some of the sting away. I wish they could've met her. Dad would've loved her sass, and Mum would've just loved that I found someone.

Jesus. Listen to me. Smitten after just a day.

"Can I ask about you?" I ask gently, knowing that since she inherited this place, it means she doesn't have any family left. "I don't want to bring up anything you don't want to talk about."

"No, it's fine." She smiles as I move to her other foot, taking off her shoe and digging my thumbs into her arch. "I lost my parents a long time ago. I had just turned eighteen, and Mom had been battling cancer for a long time. She was surrounded by love the day she went, and thankfully, she just closed her eyes and went to sleep. Dad took it hard, though."

Her voice breaks a bit, but she's strong, my girl. And she continues on with a forced smile. "They loved each other so much, you know? Dad just couldn't live without her. He left me a note, apologizing, but I've never blamed him or hated him for leaving me. They had been high school sweethearts, and he just couldn't do life without her."

Suicide. That is not what I was expecting. And I can't imagine the pain.

"But," she says, her voice returning to normal, "we did have a tradition of watching *Christmas Vacation* every year while we decorated the tree. Well, they decorated. I just ate the cookies and watched the movie."

"That's what we should do tomorrow, then. We can eat junk food and watch Christmas movies all day. How's that sound?"

Her lip quivers, dimples forming in her chin as she holds back her emotions. "That sounds amazing, actually."

I abandon her foot and pull her into my lap instead, her dress rucking up around her hips as my hands run up her thighs and over her ass. Her arms rest on my shoulders as I kiss up her throat to her jaw. "It's a date."

CHAPTER NINE
FLORENCE

CHRISTMAS Eve

After being too tired to literally do anything after dinner, we went straight to bed. And waking up next to him, but in my bed instead of a couch this time, has me a little giddy. Sure, he snores, and he's a little bit of a blanket hog, but he held me periodically through the night and got up to check on the fireplaces for me a couple of times.

So when I realize he's still asleep, I decide to crawl under the covers and wake him up the way he deserves. He's only wearing the sweatpants we found for him yesterday, and I slowly tug them down over his hips, just until I can free his soft cock. It doesn't take long to get him going, though. A few light touches, a few kisses on his hips and thighs, and he's already growing hard for me.

Briggs is a tall man, with plenty of muscles from

working on the grounds for so long, so I shouldn't have been surprised when I first saw how *large* he is. But it still caused a little jolt of fear to run down my spine. But now, it just gives me a challenge. One that I am very happy to accept. I lick from his base to his tip, where precum has already started to collect.

A soft groan comes from his chest, and then his hips begin to roll as I take him deep into my mouth. I don't have much of a gag reflex, but if anyone is going to trigger it, it's Briggs. I swallow, fighting the urge to gag when he taps the back of my throat. Then, his hands run over my arms and up into my hair, where he holds it back out of my face. The covers are pulled back, and his dark eyes lock onto mine.

"Look at you," he says, his voice rough from sleep. My clit pulses at the gruffness. "I knew you'd look so fucking pretty with your lips wrapped around my cock, princess."

Ugh, god. I love it when he calls me that.

I pop off and lick my lips as I palm him, continuing to stroke him from root to tip. "I just wanted a taste," I tell him, a coy smile playing on my lips.

When I take him again, his head falls back on the pillow, and his jaw hangs slack. I love the way I can affect him. I watch as his chest rises and falls, his abs contract, and his hips thrust. When I run my hand up over his stomach and onto his chest, he grabs hold of it, hanging on tight as I continue to work him into a frenzy.

It doesn't take long before he's pulling me up on top

of him. My pussy is soaked, and I roll my hips as we kiss and kiss and kiss. His cock slips between my lower lips and strokes my clit in the best way. Pleasure builds low in my belly as he tugs my oversized shirt over my head and tosses it to the side. His arms wrap around me, holding me close as he rolls to his side.

My leg wraps around his hip while we continue to lazily kiss and explore each other's bodies. The other night was a collision of overwhelming tension and passion that neither one of us could stop. But this is slow and sensual. We're taking our time together, getting to know what the other one likes and how. His hands run all over my body, his nails tickling my back and arms, while I focus on pulling him as close as possible, my fingers digging into the hard muscles of his ass and thighs.

The tip of his cock presses against my entrance, and he teases me, thrusting just enough to slip it in and out, over and over again. His dark eyes lock onto my own, and one of his annoying little smirks plays on his lips as one of his hands grabs hold of my ass. He spreads me further and then presses slowly inside of me. My mouth drops open, my eyes close, and I let my forehead rest against his as he fills me so fully.

"This what you wanted, Ren?" he asks as he bottoms out inside of me.

I nod, brushing my lips against his, and then work my hips to make him fucking *move*.

"Eager, eager," he whispers, a breathy laugh escaping his mouth.

But he gives me what I want anyway, pulling out and pushing back in, his cock hitting that same sweet spot he discovered last time. Briggs holds me tightly, kissing me in between breaths and whispering sweet nothings that turn my insides to jelly. The pleasure that was building earlier is back, and it coils tightly until I'm afraid he might actually break me this time.

And yet, I don't. He works me through it, building me up and giving me a safe space to fall apart.

"My god, you are stunning," he tells me as I cry out his name, my muscles fluttering and pulsing around him. "I want to watch you like this forever." He kisses my cheeks and my jaw, nipping at my lips before looping his arm under my leg, lifting it higher for a better angle.

"I wouldn't fight you on that," I tease, my voice breathy from the orgasm I'm still coming down from.

"Yeah?" he asks, his hips beginning to pick up the pace, almost slamming into me each time. It's hard to catch my breath or even keep my eyes open. The pleasure is an assault on my senses. "You want me to take you like this every morning?" he continues. "Eat you for lunch, then bend you over the table for dinner?"

"Oh, god," I gasp as that slight curve in his cock hits an even deeper spot.

"That's my girl," he coos. "Come with me. Show me just how much you need this."

I hold his face, our eyes locked on one another's, and let the rest of the world fade into the background. Right now, it's just me and Briggs, enjoying each other's bodies and company. It's just us in this secret little snowed-in world. There's no one watching us to see what will happen, no one to gossip to, no one to make me second-guess myself. There's just us and this moment we're in.

As both of us come, we hold on to each other. It's probably the most intimate moment I've ever shared with another person. If I let the anxious voice in the back of my head have control, I'll start to panic that this is all happening too fast—too soon. But we agreed we're on the same page, so I push all of those thoughts away and just enjoy the feeling of connecting with him.

AFTER LYING in bed together until almost lunchtime, we decided to watch Christmas movies like my parents and I used to do. There was no decorating any of the Christmas trees, since that had all been done before I got here, but he did find cookie dough in the fridge. And for premade dough, those things were amazing.

As the day went on, we decided to dig through the several deep freezers in the back of the home—which, why do we have so many, may I ask?—hoping to find a good amount of ingredients that we could make a Christmas dinner with. Briggs tells me that the plows won't really bother with working until after Boxing Day, so we're definitely stuck here until the twenty-seventh.

Not to worry, though, because we have four deep freezers full of food.

Apparently, my great-aunt was a bit of a hoarder.

"We always do pizza on Christmas Eve," Briggs says, lifting a turkey the size of a small toddler out of the chest freezer. "And while I love this time with you, I think I'd kill for a Christmas Eve pizza right about now."

I laugh, pulling out a frozen bag of rolls from the one I'm digging through. "With all this food, we can surely find the shit to make a pizza or two. I know I saw marinara in the pantry and some fresh mozzarella in the fridge."

We carry all of our findings back to the kitchen, laying everything out on the table. Between the pantry and the freezers, we found turkey, stuffing, cranberry sauce, rolls, and one lonesome blackberry pie that Briggs swears has been there for at least a year. I'm not complaining, though. It's been frozen, so whatever. I just want some pie.

"Also," he says, smirking as he walks over to where I've hopped up onto a counter, "I may not have found any pizza dough, but I did find..." He whips out a red-and-yellow box. "Garlic bread!"

"I used to make these when I was in college," I tell him. "Mini pizzas made out of garlic bread?" I kiss my fingers. "Perfection when you come in late from a night out."

"Oh, yeah?" He tosses the box onto the counter next to me and then cages me in with his arms. I'm just taller than him from this angle, and I lean forward to rest on my palms, putting us back on the same eye level. "You a party girl, little duck?"

"Now?" I laugh, placing my forearms on his shoulders and playing with his hair that brushes his neck. "God, no. When I hit twenty-five, my body just stopped accepting alcohol. It was like overnight I couldn't hold it any longer. I'd throw up almost every time."

I make a face, and he mimics it, scrunching his nose and barely containing a laugh. "I was never really a big drinker." He shrugs. "I'd go out and get some beers with my friends every once in a while, but Dad was a nightmare at times. I knew I had to be at this place bright and early five days a week, even when I was a teen, and a hangover from my off days would not be a good enough excuse to get out of it."

He smiles at the memories, while they sound awful to me because, if I'm honest, I was spoiled as hell. I was my parents' only child, so they coddled the hell out of me. I don't think I had a job until I went to college. Mom always told me I needed to get one in high school to help pay for my car and the insurance for it, but Dad was such a pushover that it was never enforced. So to know Briggs was working his ass off even as a teenager kind of makes me sad for him.

"Doesn't sound like a lot of fun was had," I say, the twinge of pity showing in my tone.

"Ah," he says, dismissing the thought. "It might not have always been at the time, but looking back, I'm glad

I got all that time with him." Briggs smiles and leans in for a soft kiss. "I take it you were the spoiled angel child?"

My head falls forward as I laugh. "Yes." I pull back and shake my head, rolling my eyes. "Of course, I would never complain about how I grew up. I know I was very privileged, and clearly still very much am. But I do wish they had forced me to do a bit more than they did. When I lost both of them, I suddenly realized I didn't know shit about fuck all."

"Shit about fuck all," he repeats, his voice filled with humor. He grabs my hands, folding our fingers together. "That's a new one."

"It's true!" He steps between my legs and brings one of my hands to his lips, kissing my knuckles as I speak. "I didn't know the first thing about taxes, interest rates on credit cards, or how to even fill out a W-2 for my job!"

"What's a W-2?" he asks, his brow pulling together.

"It's a thing Americans have to fill out for the IRS. Estimates how much they should be taking out of our paycheck, shows them that we're legal to work, et cetera." I shrug. "I think, anyway. I still don't fully know."

He kisses the inside of my wrist and looks up at me from under his annoyingly long eyelashes, making the butterflies in my belly start fluttering again. "Good thing you have me, then, eh?" His grin is frustratingly handsome. I swear, every time he smiles, it just transforms his entire face. "I'll keep you in line over here, make sure you don't run this place into the ground."

I scoff, shoving him in the chest as he laughs. "I'll have you know that I read every single document the lawyers gave me." I look down my nose at him, holding back my own smile. "My roommate even made me flash cards so that I could memorize certain things."

He softly touches my face and then cups either side, his eyes bouncing back and forth between my own. "I have not a single shred of doubt, Florence Donahue, that you will be amazing in this new phase of your life."

It's so sincere and said in such an intimate way that I have to swallow at the sudden pain in my throat and blink back the tears that start to form. I can't remember the last time someone so wholeheartedly believed in me. And to know it's someone who has only known me for a few days makes a pretty big impact.

I lean into him, kissing him roughly on the lips before whispering, "Thank you, Briggs."

He just smiles and captures my mouth again.

CHAPTER TEN

BRIGGS

Ren thinks I'm getting up to check on the fires throughout the night, which is true. I am. I wouldn't normally leave them burning for so long, but this storm is a fucking monster, and I don't want the radiators to struggle to keep up. But this time, I'm actually going to sneak down to the den and make her a stocking.

I hate that I'm not able to get out of here and get her a gift, but just because I can't do that doesn't mean I can't try to make her first Christmas in England a special one. I'm not sure if it's that fact that I'm exhausted because it's damn near four in the morning or if we've just somehow misplaced the stockings that Katharine, Ren's great-aunt, used every year. I even climbed up into the damn attic, searching for the things. It's a wonder that Ren hasn't gotten up to look for me.

So, socks it is.

I laugh to myself as I pull my clean socks out of the tumble dryer and then make my way to the pantry. It's full of snacks and sweets since Mary does most of the shopping and has a sweet tooth like I've never seen. She always claims that she buys all that stuff for the kids that run around the estate in the summers, but that doesn't explain why she has to restock through the winter.

"This will have to do until I can get to the shops," I whisper as I pull chocolates and sweets from the hidden stash. Even though the socks I was wearing the other day are tall and thick, it's still a struggle to fit a ton of stuff in them. But, oh well. It's the thought that counts, right?

Moving back to the den, I lay the "stockings" under the tree in the far corner. Whoever thought hanging them above a burning fireplace was fucking insane. Not only is that a serious fire hazard, but all the chocolate would melt. I smile to myself and then take a moment to breathe in the Christmas joy. I miss my sister and her little minions, but I don't think my heart has felt this light in years—decades, maybe. It's an intense feeling, knowing that someone who could be the love of my life is right upstairs, waiting to celebrate her first Christmas in England.

I'm trying not to let myself move too quickly. I mean, shit, we've not even known each other a week. And I know how crazy that sounds. When I took a few minutes to call my sister earlier today—well, yesterday now, I guess—she interrogated me like I was on trial for murder.

"Guard that heart of yours," she said. "I know how hard it is for you to find someone you can actually stand to be around, so this is big news." The laughter was very clear in her voice. "But it also means you might jump in too quickly, and I don't want you getting hurt."

She was right; it has been hard to find anyone I can stand to be around for the long haul. Some might call me picky, but I just never wanted to settle for someone who wasn't going to give me everything I needed out of a partner. But Florence is different; I can feel it in my damn bones. The way she looks at me, speaks to me and *listens*. I promised Tess that I'd behave, that I'd treat her well while also protecting my own heart.

I just don't think I really need to, is all.

"No, you didn't!" Ren squeals, covering up her laughing as she looks at my clean socks stuffed with sweets. I even made sure there was Christmas music playing on the TV in the background. Really proud of the scene I set, I must say. "Please tell me those are not your socks."

I grin at her and shrug. "Couldn't find the stockings, so I decided to make do with what we had."

"Amazing," she says, snorting with laughter as she walks over to the tree. She sinks down and crosses her legs, an impressive feat that my old knees could never accomplish. "Come on, then." She gestures for me to come sit down next to her. I do, but it's a bit slower.

"When did you do this?" she asks, her eyes wide with delight as she begins to dig through the chocolates.

"When I got up last night to check the fireplaces. I really figured I'd be able to find the stockings somewhere, but I swear I left no stone unturned and couldn't find a single one. Even went up to the creepy attic."

"How in the world did I not hear you?" She pulls out the Terry's Chocolate Orange and then suddenly throws her arms around my shoulders, pulling me close in an aggressive fashion. "Thank you," she whispers when we both finally stop laughing. "Thank you so much, Briggs."

"Hey, hey." I tug her into my lap, holding her close and rubbing circles on her back as she buries her face in my neck. "It's okay, Ren, really. It was nothing. Just some sweets in my socks."

She pulls back a little, making sure she can look me in the eyes as her hands rest on my shoulders and her thumbs run along the edge of my jaw. Which reminds me, I really need a trim. The beard is getting out of control.

"I don't think you understand," she says, her voice filled with emotion. "Do you realize that you could've just not done anything? Like when you couldn't find the stockings, you could've just abandoned the idea. But you didn't. You filled your damn *socks*." Another snort of laughter. "Honestly, even you trying to find the stockings

is huge. I've always had to drop hints or beg my ex-part-
ners to do fun, romantic things with me."

I hum and play with her hair that falls over one of her
shoulders. It's messy from sleep and all the fun things I
kept her up doing last night, but she's so beautiful like
this. The sun is out, helping to melt some of the snow
and shining through the window and onto the tree. The
warm light of the fire flickers across her features as she
tries her best not to cry.

"Is that what we are, princess?" I ask, finding the
courage I didn't think I'd have so soon. "Partners?"

"Would you like to be?" she questions, looking at me
from under those pretty, blonde eyelashes.

I take a breath, attempting to steady my heart, which
seems to be trying to break free. "I think I'd like to be," I
admit as I try to hold her gaze. I don't want her to think I
don't want this in any way. I do. I really, really want this.
But I'll understand if it's too quick for her.

"Are you trying to ask me out, Mr. Davies?" Her
eyes are playful now, and I pull her even closer, my
palms resting on her perfect ass. "Because if so, I think
you should just come right out with it."

I shake my head back and forth slowly, grinning from
ear to ear at how this is playing out. "Miss Florence
Dona—"

"Anne," she interrupts. "Anne is my middle name."

"Miss Florence *Anne* Donahue," I correct as she
nods. "Would you like to go steady?"

Her head falls back for a moment, my favorite laugh

of hers exploding through her. "I think I'd like that very much, Mr. Briggs…?"

"Oh, I'd rather not," I grimace as I nervously laugh. Eugene is not a name you brag about.

"You have an embarrassing middle name?" She lights up at the idea. "Oh, that's great, honestly. Because you're too amazing. It's good to know you at least have one thing about you that isn't so *perfect*."

"I am *not* perfect by any means—"

"Shh," she says, pressing a finger over my lips, her smile ornery as hell. "You don't have to tell me now. In fact," Ren continues, her hands roaming over my cheeks and back into my hair, "I think I'd like to thank you properly for the Christmas stockings, anyway." She grins and shrugs. "Before you ruin it with your horrendous middle name."

I begin to give her a piece of my mind, but her pouty lips cut me off as she leans in and kisses me. Our mouths open, and our tongues dance together while our hands explore each other's bodies. She fits against me like she was always meant to be here, and it sends a pang of sadness through me that my parents will never get to meet her. Because, damn, they would adore her.

Who knew that I, grumpy-as-shit Briggs Davies, would fall for an American woman. It's all very King Edward the Eighth of me.

"Merry Christmas," she whispers against my mouth as our kisses slow.

And as I sit here, my woman in my arms, the fireplace warming the den, and "It's Beginning To Look A Lot Like Christmas" playing in the background, I realize just how happy I am that the old Rover got stuck. Happy that the snowstorm came, happy that it was *me* who offered to pick her up, happy that she came down to the kitchen that night—even if it did get me kneed in the nuts.

I smile as I kiss her again and again.

"Happy Christmas, Florence."

EPILOGUE
FLORENCE

NEW YEAR'S Eve

"You look *so* nervous," Briggs teases as he squeezes my hand. We're sitting in the driveway of his sister's home, and it's freaking gorgeous. It's a two-story cottage with swags and red bows on every window. There's an orange glow coming from the downstairs windows, and I can see shadows moving behind the curtains.

And, yes, Briggs is right. I am nervous.

I nod and lick my lips, then fret I've fucked up my lipstick and pull down the small mirror to check a little too roughly. It clunks against the windshield, and Briggs leans over, grasping my face in his hands. I'm forced to turn away from my reflected face and look at him.

"They're going to love you, little duck." He kisses the tip of my nose. "It will be okay, I promise."

"I just really want them to like me," I admit, my voice cracking into a whisper. I know this is probably crazy. I shouldn't be this worried about meeting my boyfriend's family. But my anxiety always plays up in social situations, and I really wish Amie's flight hadn't been postponed until after the new year. The same storm that brought me Briggs delayed her flight. I could really use her right now, just to help take the pressure off.

"They will, sweet girl." His smile is reassuring, and I try to pull myself together. They'll definitely not like me if I'm an anxious, bumbling mess.

"Okay," I say, taking a steeling breath. "Let's do this."

Briggs grins, kisses me once on the cheek, and then hops out of the Rover, running at a decent clip around the hood to open my door. "Surprised you didn't eat it just then," I tell him, laughing as he lifts me down out of the car. "It's still icy."

While this is a New Year's Eve party, it's just the six of us. They told Briggs they wanted me all to themselves so they wouldn't be inviting anyone else over. It's a relief because I did not feel like dressing up to the nines in this frigid weather. So instead, I've paired my favorite jeans with a thick green sweater and a pair of snow boots. I curled my hair and put on a little makeup just to make a good first impression.

He holds on to me tightly as we walk over the salted driveway and up to the doorstep. It's made of the prettiest old stone, and Tess has decorated it beautifully. There's a skinny tree with fake presents all around it and a large Christmas wreath on the heavy front door. Briggs knocks a couple of times, then opens the door, letting the warmth from inside defrost my nose.

"Just us!" he calls out as we step inside. I can hear the kids laughing and music playing. And the unmistakable smell of pizza wafts into my nose.

"Pizza," I groan as he takes off my coat. It's the first time we've really been able to leave the estate since I got here, and pizza reminds me so much of home that I could cry.

"They said the kids wanted to treat this like Christmas Eve since I couldn't make it on the real day," Briggs answers with a warm smile. I can tell he loves those kids with all his heart. "Thought it would make a nice surprise for you."

"Coming!" booms a voice from down the hall.

"Sorry!" says a woman, who I assume is Tess, as she comes out of the back room. Her hair is tied up in a messy bun, and she's wearing a stained sweatshirt and leggings with fluffy socks on her feet. "Florence!" she squeals, her face breaking out in the most genuine smile.

"Told you not to dress up," Briggs whispers just before I'm engulfed in Tess' arms.

"What did you whisper to her?" she asks as she holds me close. "Talking out your arse about me?"

I laugh, immediately feeling at ease. She pulls back, giving Briggs a look before turning back into the happy woman who hugged me. "It's so nice to meet you, Florence. Please, don't listen to a word Briggs has to say about us. I promise you it's all bollocks."

"I've not said a single nasty thing, I'll have you know," he says haughtily.

"He really hasn't," I say with a shrug. "I've actually been very nervous to meet you."

"As if, love. Never be nervous. And look at you!" She holds my hands out to our sides as she gives me a once-over. "Beautiful. Come, let me introduce you to Dom and the twins."

"We're the twins!" they both announce as they step into our line of sight.

"There's the little shites!" Briggs shouts as they both start to run toward him, laughing and screaming. He squats down, and they both tackle him to the ground.

Tess rolls her eyes and ignores them, tugging me down the hall until we're in the kitchen. "This is Florence," she announces. "Florence, this is my husband, Dom."

He has an apron on while he stands at the counter, cutting up some fruit. "So nice to meet you, Florence," he says, pausing quickly to wipe his hand before offering it to me.

"You guys can call me Ren," I tell them as I shake his hand. "Thanks for having us both over tonight."

"Of course!" Tess grabs some plates from the cabinet, and I immediately take them from her. "Thank you," she says with a sigh, using her now free hands to grab a roll of paper towels and a couple of boxes of pizza. "The table is just through here."

I follow her through the archway and lay the plates

out around the table. Briggs and the twins come into the dining room as we're finishing, and all three come straight over to me.

"Twin One and Twin Two," Briggs says, a hand on each of their shoulders. "Introduce yourselves."

"Hi, I'm Maya," a little girl with dark, wispy bangs says as she steps forward, her small hand outstretched toward me.

"Hello, Maya." I squat down to their level. "You can call me Ren. It's lovely to meet you."

"And I am Oliver, but I actually prefer to be called Oli because it's less to say." He holds out his hand as well, gently pushing away his sister's hand. Maya just rolls her eyes and walks over to Tess, tugging on her sweatshirt.

"Lovely to meet you, Oli," I say with a smile, trying not to grimace at how warm and damp his hand is. Like I said, not a kid person.

After the formalities are finished, Oli and Maya both climb up into their chairs and watch their mother cut up their pieces of pizza. Briggs wraps me up in his arms, and I take the opportunity to discreetly wipe my hand on the back of his shirt.

"Sticky hands," I whisper, making him chuckle.

"Gross, right?" he asks, scrunching up his nose.

"Sit, sit!" Dom encourages as he walks in with bowls of cut-up strawberries and apples. "One for Oli and one for Maya," he says, sitting them down next to their plates of pizza.

"None of the adults have fruit," Oli points out as Briggs pulls a chair out for me.

"Very good observation," Dom tells him.

This must be enough for Oli because he just shrugs before shoving a whole apple slice in his mouth. Maya does the same, except with a strawberry.

"Maya is always trying to be different these days," Briggs whispers when he takes his seat next to me. "They used to do everything the same, even at the same time. But I think she's going through a *boys are annoying* phase and doesn't want to be lumped into that."

"Boys *are* annoying," Maya grumbles, having heard what her uncle said.

"Yeah, well, girls have germs, so…"

"Girls have no more germs than boys do, Oliver," Tess says, the annoyance in her voice clear. "We've talked about this."

"Do you like Uncle Briggs?" Oli asks, ignoring his mother and looking straight at me. A lesser person would wither under that stare he's giving me.

"I do," I tell him, pausing to thank Briggs as he throws two slices of pepperoni pizza on my plate. I'm going to have to figure out how to get ranch over here. How in the world do these people eat pizza without ranch? "He's pretty great, right?"

Oli nods and then goes right back to ignoring everyone as he digs into his pizza, covering his face and fingers in red sauce.

When I look back to the table, I notice everyone

passing a jar of mayonnaise around. Briggs scoops a spoonful out and plops it onto his plate. I look at him in complete horror.

"You all are not going to do what I think you're going to do," I say, looking around at everyone's plates. Of course, they all look at me like I've lost my mind. "Are you about to dip your pizza in mayo?"

Briggs snorts to my left. "Americans."

I whip my head in his direction and narrow my eyes. "Rude."

But because I'm not a party pooper, I let him scoop some mayonnaise out onto my plate as well. One tentative bite later, and I have to admit, it's actually pretty good. Everyone laughs and goes back to chatting while Briggs leans in close, kissing my temple before whispering, "See? Just needed to have a taste. Just like with me."

He winks, and if we were alone, he would be paying for that comment.

"Tell us about yourself, Ren," Dom says, interrupting our little moment. "Besides being stuck alone with this man for the past week, how're you enjoying your new home so far?"

"Not to inflate his already large ego," I say with a smile, rolling my eyes when Briggs winks yet again, "but he's kind of been great. And it's probably because of him that I'm not catching the first flight home."

They all laugh, but I'm kind of serious. If I had been stuck in that house all by myself for the week of Christmas, I don't think I would've made it out the other side. Talk about a depressing way to spend your Christmas.

They continue to ask me questions, genuinely seeming interested in learning about my life, and when it gets late, they excuse themselves to put the kids to bed. The twins both complain, but they're yawning as they're carried upstairs.

The night is filled with laughs, games, and stories told about Briggs growing up. We have the TV on in the background, the hosts of the show in London counting down the hours and then minutes until the ball drops. All four of us ring in the new year together, each of us with just a single glass of champagne so that Briggs is safe to drive us home.

And after sharing a kiss with Briggs as the ball drops, we help Dom and Tess clean up and then gather our things. I excuse myself to the bathroom, and before I come out, I hear Tess talking to Briggs in the hallway.

"She's lovely," Tess whispers. "Absolutely perfect for you."

"Isn't she?" I can hear the smile in his voice. "It's been fast, but it's been…" He pauses, and I can hear shuffling.

"They'd be so thrilled for you, Briggsy," Tess tells him, and I have to fight back the urge to crumple into tears. Hearing that from her was the confirmation I needed and more. To know that she likes me and that their parents would have, too, is too much for my hope-less-romantic self.

"Don't be a stranger," Dom tells me as I finally open the door, joining them all in the foyer.

"Please don't. It's been lovely having you," Tess agrees, pulling me in for another tight hug.

We say our goodbyes and trek back out into the cold, Briggs' arm around my shoulders, his head tilted back as he smiles toward the night sky.

"I knew they'd love you," he says, grinning from ear to ear. The moon shines down, illuminating our path and the soft lines on his handsome face.

"Oh, yeah?" I ask, a hint of sarcasm to my tone. "And how'd you know that?"

He pauses, opens the passenger door for me, and then smiles and shrugs, like it's the most obvious thing in the world.

"Because I love you, Florence."

WANT TO READ MORE
FROM THE NAUGHTY
AND SPICE WORLD?

SEE THE SERIES PAGE HERE!

A few more by Dana Isaly...

Nick and Holly Series

The One Night Series

As Above So Below

Into The Dark

About the Author

Dana Isaly is a International Bestselling Romance author that has dipped her toes in dark, paranormal, and even romcom.

She was born in the midwest, grew up in the south, went to university in England, and even spent a couple years in California. She is a lover of books, coffee, and rainy days.

She swears too much, loves dogs more than people, and believes that love is love is love.

You can find her on Instagram (@author.danaisaly) or join her Facebook group (Dana's House of Horny Humans).